For La Virgencita de la Altagracia, thank you and *gracias* for all your blessings!

—J.A.

This one is for Morgan, my dearest goddaughter.

—B.V.

THIS IS A BORZOI BOOK PUBLISHED BY ALFRED A. KNOPF
Text copyright © 2005 by Julia Alvarez
Illustrations copyright © 2005 by Beatriz Vidal
All rights reserved under International and Pan-American Copyright
Conventions. Published in the United States by Alfred A. Knopf, an imprint of
Random House Children's Books, a division of Random House, Inc.,
New York, and simultaneously in Canada by
Random House of Canada Limited, Toronto.
Distributed by Random House, Inc., New York.
www.randomhouse.com/kids
KNOPF, BORZOI BOOKS, and the colophon are registered trademarks of
Random House, Inc.

Library of Congress Cataloging-in-Publication Data
Alvarez, Julia.
A gift of gracias : the legend of Altagracia / written by Julia Alvarez ;
illustrated by Beatriz Vidal. — 1st ed.
p.   cm.
SUMMARY: María's family is almost forced to leave their farm on the new island
colony, until a mysterious lady appears in María's dream.
ISBN 0-375-82425-1 (trade) — ISBN 0-375-92425-6 (lib. bdg.)
[1. Oranges—Fiction. 2. Christian patron saints—Fiction. 3. Dominican
Republic—Fiction.] I. Vidal, Beatriz, ill. II. Title.
PZ7.A48Gi 2005
[E]—dc22
2004025397

MANUFACTURED IN MALAYSIA
October 2005
10 9 8 7 6 5 4 3 2 1
First Edition

A Gift of Gracias

A Gift of Gracias

THE LEGEND OF ALTAGRACIA

WRITTEN BY
JULIA ALVAREZ

ILLUSTRATED BY
BEATRIZ VIDAL

ALFRED A. KNOPF
NEW YORK

"María!" her mother called up. "Do you see them?"

María had climbed on the roof. Her father and the old Indian Quisqueya were not back from the city yet. What could have happened to them?

"No, Mamá," María called softly down.
The orange sun was sinking below the horizon.

Before he left on his journey, Papá had asked María what gift he could bring her.

María knew the *finca* was not doing well. Papá and his farmer friends were trying to grow olives like they had in Spain. But olive trees did not flourish in this new land.

"Just come back safely, Papá," María had said. With the poor harvests all around, desperate *bandidos* were holding up travelers on the road.

That night, as María lay in the dark, she whispered, "Remember my gift, Papá."

The next morning, Papá and Quisqueya were waiting at the table!

María gave each a warm smile. "You kept your promise, Papá, thank you!"

Papá laughed. "I have something else for you." He nodded toward a basket of golden fruit.

María stared in wonder. "What are they?"

"Oranges, like the ones your mother and I used to eat in Valencia, Spain."

María had never been to Spain. Her parents often talked of their homeland. But they had never mentioned "oranges."

"A merchant gave them to Quisqueya and me for helping unload them at the market." Papá peeled off the golden rind. He handed María a piece.

It smelled sharp and fresh, like tickling inside her nose. It tasted like a sweet sunrise, tingling inside her mouth.

While they ate the oranges, Papá told stories of the wonders he had seen in the city.

"Would you like to live there?" Papá asked María when he had finished.

"You mean, leave the farm?"

Papá nodded sadly. "The farm is not prospering, as you know."

María bowed her head. Tears fell on the seeds she had collected in her bowl.
Don't worry, María, Quisqueya whispered. *We will find a way to stay.* His
golden face glowed like an indoor sun.

That night, María dreamed that she was holding a bowl of orange seeds. One by one, she was planting them in the ground. As she did, she heard Quisqueya's voice whispering in her ear, *Say gracias.*

"Thank you," María obeyed.

As she said so, María felt her heart fill with sweetness. *"Muchas gracias,"* she whispered, more sincerely. Many thanks.

Suddenly, as if these were magic words, trees burst out of the ground full of leafy branches heavy with oranges. Under the grove stood a beautiful lady with golden skin and a crown of stars.

"Who are you?" María gasped.

"I am called Nuestra Señora de la Altagracia," the lady said. Our Lady of Thanks.

In the darkness, the lady's robe twinkled with hundreds of stars.

Above her, the branches had woven a roof hung with hundreds of small suns.

The next morning, María woke up early. She wanted to catch Papá and Quisqueya before they left for the fields.

"I know what will grow on the farm!" María recounted her dream of the beautiful lady in a grove of orange trees.

"Oranges?" Papá murmured thoughtfully, and looked over at Quisqueya.
The old man nodded. His eyes shone with a special light.
That very day, the family began planting. They put seeds in the ground and
said *gracias*.

And those seeds sprouted into shoots that grew into trunks that spread into branches filled with oranges that glowed like little suns.

In a matter of months, trees that would normally take years to grow yielded a large crop. Papá and Quisqueya were ready to carry a load to the city.

The morning of his journey, Papá thanked María for saving the farm. "These oranges will sell for many gold coins. Now I can bring you back a real gift. Ask for anything you want."

María could not think of anything she wanted more than to see the beautiful lady, night and day. To say *gracias* and feel that sweetness in her heart again.

"Please bring me a portrait of Our Lady of Altagracia."

Every night that Papá and Quisqueya were gone, María had a dream. She could see all that had happened that day in the city as if she were with them.

She saw her father arriving at the market with his wagonload of oranges. She saw the gold coins falling into Papá's hands.

María saw her father going from stall to stall asking for a picture of Our Lady of Altagracia. She saw the merchants shaking their heads no.

Finally, her father and Quisqueya set out for home. When night fell, they unrolled their blankets. Soon Papá was asleep. But Quisqueya sat up, watching the sky. The stars were moving slowly, outlining a lady's face smiling down at him.

Suddenly the stars shot down toward the earth below: a shower of light
in the middle of the night!

Quisqueya stood and held out the blanket that had been covering his shoulders.
He tried to catch the stars before they hit the ground.

While Papá and Quisqueya were gone, María and her mother tried to keep up with the oranges. They were dropping to the ground and spoiling.

"I hope Papá and Quisqueya come soon," Mamá said, "or we will lose this harvest."

The evening of their return, Quisqueya and Papá were full of happy news. The oranges had sold in a matter of hours.

"But we could not find Our Lady of Altagracia anywhere, María," Papá said sadly.

"We could not find her in the city," the old Indian agreed. "But on the way home, I looked up at the sky and saw the lady who for ages has taken care of my people."

Quisqueya unrolled his blanket, and there, as if painted on the cloth, was a picture of the beautiful lady.

"That's the lady in my dream! Our Lady of Altagracia!" María dropped to her knees beside Mamá and Papá and gave thanks.

Papá gazed out at the hundreds of oranges growing in the orchard. "We'd better pick them now or they will drop and spoil!"

"But it will soon be too dark." María pointed. The sun was sinking below the horizon.

"Do not worry," Quisqueya reminded her. "Our Lady will find a way."

Quisqueya hung the blanket with the lady's picture from an orange bough.

By the light of the twinkling stars on the robe of Altagracia, María and her family picked all the oranges that night.

"*Gracias,* Altagracia," a tired María whispered. She took down the beautiful picture and draped it over her arm. From now on, Altagracia would always be by her side.

As María headed down the dark path, the stars on Our Lady's robe lighted her way.

About the Story

Many people are devoted to an image of the Virgin Mary as she has appeared in their homeland: Our Lady of Guadalupe in Mexico, Our Lady of Fátima in Portugal, Our Lady of Caridad in Cuba.

In the Dominican Republic, my native country, our special little virgin, or *virgencita*, is Our Lady of Altagracia (al-ta-GRA-see-ah). Legend says she appeared in the early 1500s, when the whole island was still a colony of Spain. So beloved is she that her saint's day, January 21, is a national holiday. I was named Julia Altagracia, and so when I was a little girl, my family would tell me the legend of Altagracia. What I have written is based on those stories.

Along with the story, my mother told me how the *virgencita* picture disappeared from the little girl's house and was found hanging from an orange bough. The family understood that the *virgencita* preferred the orchard, so a chapel was built for her among the orange trees. Pilgrims from all over the country visit her there. In fact, before I started writing this story, I traveled to the chapel in what is now the town of Higüey (ee-GWAY) to ask for her special help.

Just like me, many little girls in the Dominican Republic are named after Nuestra Señora de la Altagracia, a name that means Our Lady of High Grace, or simply, Our Lady of Thanks. As for the old Indian Quisqueya (kees-KAY-yah), that is the name the Taino Indians gave the island before the Spaniards renamed it Hispaniola, or Little Spain. Quisqueya means *La madre de la tierra*, Mother of the Earth. The native Tainos saw their own powerful Mother of the Earth in the image of Our Lady of Altagracia. Many farmers in the Dominican Republic are especially attached to Our Lady of Altagracia because of her connection with the land.

So, you see, whether you are Dominican or not, Our Lady of Thanks, like Mother Earth, really belongs to all of us.